BLACKBERRY FARM

SAM SPARROW

Jane Pilgrim

This edition first published in the United Kingdom in 2000 by
Brockhampton Press
20 Bloomsbury Street
London WC1B 3QA
a member of the Caxton Publishing Group

© Text copyright MCMLII by Jane Pilgrim
© Illustrations copyright MCMLII by Hodder & Stoughton Ltd

Reprint 2002

Designed and Produced for Brockhampton Press by
Open Door Limited
Rutland, UK

Illustrator: F. Stocks May
Colour separation: GA Graphics Stamford

Title: BLACKBERRY FARM, Sam Sparrow
ISBN: 1-84186-043-3

Printed in Singapore by Star Standard Industries Pte. Ltd.

SAM SPARROW

Jane Pilgrim

Illustrated by F. Stocks May

BROCKHAMPTON PRESS

S am Sparrow was tired. He had had a long, busy day working in his shop in London. Every day was long and busy, and every day he was tired. "I must get away from it all," he said.

So the next day he did not open
his little shop high up above
London, but flew off miles away
into the country – all the way to
Blackberry Farm.

It was nearly dark when he arrived, and all he could see was Ernest Owl watching the day turn to night. "Good evening sir," he said. "I am Sam Sparrow. I want to live at Blackberry Farm and open a little shop. Will that be all right?" Ernest Owl blinked in surprise. "Well, well young man!" he hooted. "I must think. Come back in the morning."

Next morning Sam Sparrow returned to Ernest Owl's oak-tree where he met Joe Robin, Mrs Squirrel and Lucy Mouse. Ernest Owl introduced him. "My friend Sam Sparrow from London," he said. "He wants to open a shop at Blackberry Farm, and I think it is a good idea." the others thought so too, but where was it to be?

Lucy Mouse showed him a very good corner in the stable, but that was too low down. Mrs Squirrel begged him to move into the big beech tree next door to her. But that was too high up.

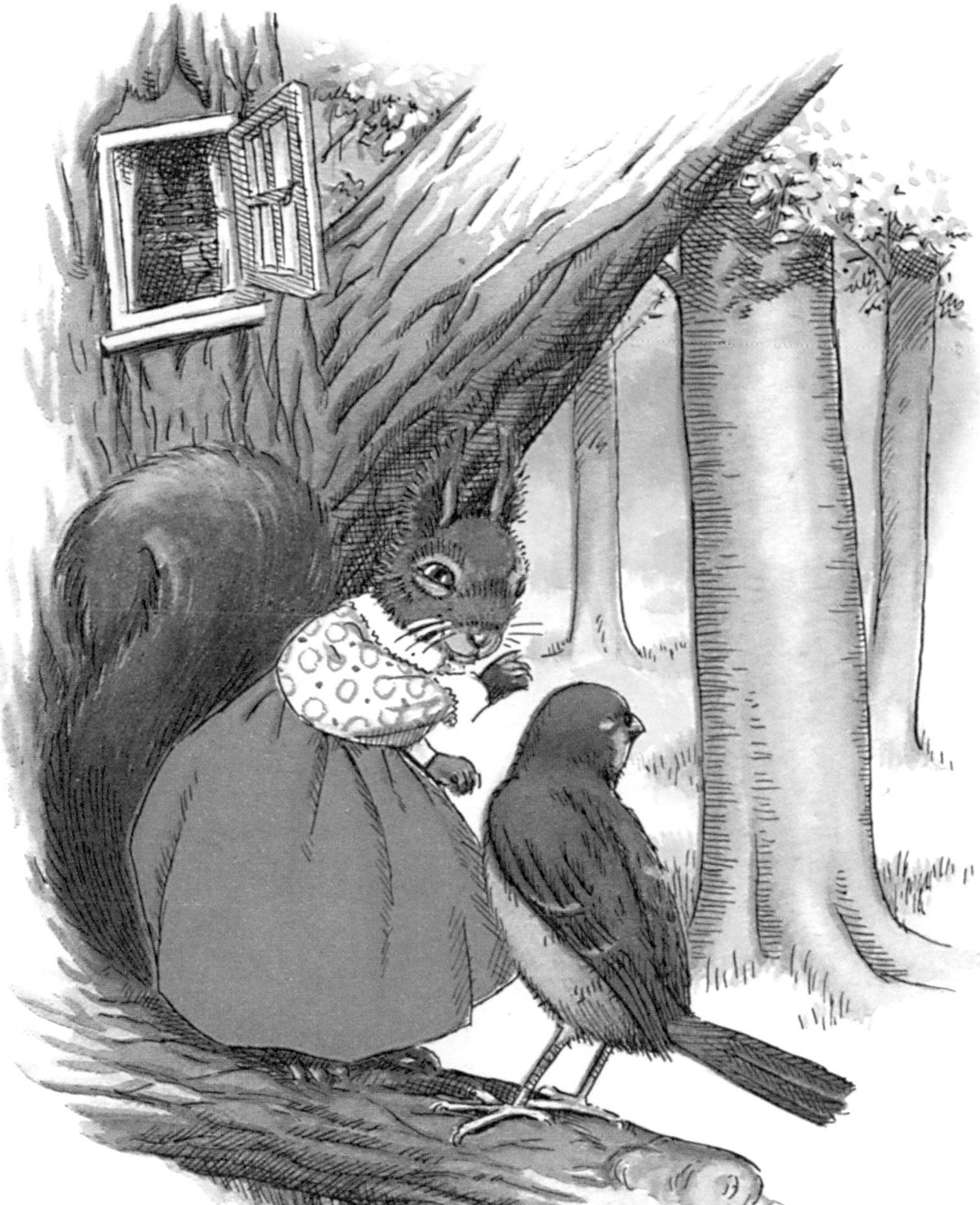

Joe Robin showed him the old
window above the barn door. But
that was too small.

Sam did not think that any of those were quite right, and he chose an old box on a bench under the wall near the barn. As he perched on his new home, he said, "It must not be too high up. It must not be too low down. It must be just right for everyone."

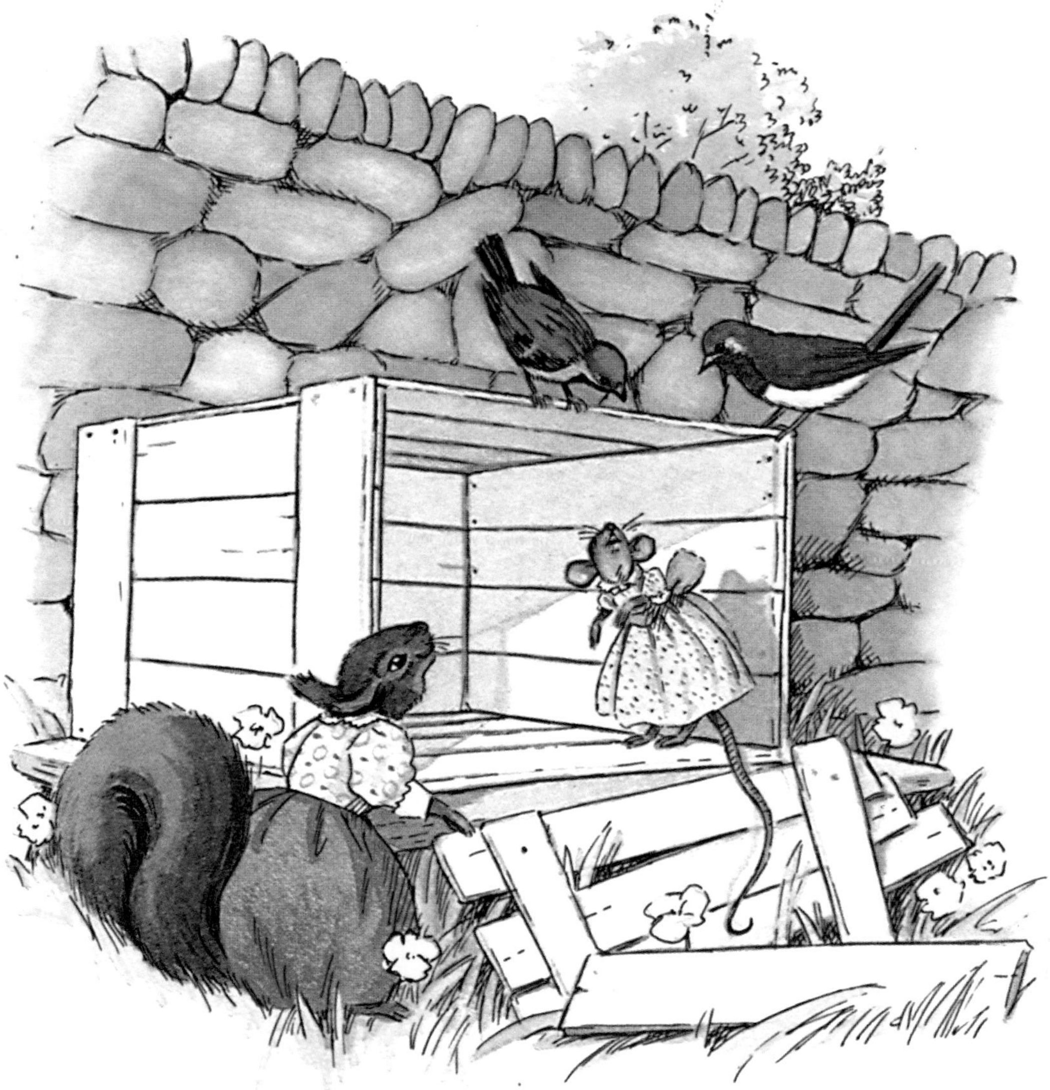

All that day, and all the next day,
and all the next, he worked to get
his shop ready. Lucy Mouse
brought Mother Hen to help.

Mr Nibble put up shelves, Mrs Nibble made curtains, and Sam Sparrow wrote long lists of all the things his shop should keep. He gave the letter to Joe Robin, because Joe Robin was Postman Joe of Blackberry Farm.

Three days later the goods arrived, flown in by Starling and Sons of London. Sam was delighted. "How quick you have been," he told Mr Starling, who bowed and thanked him for the order and accepted the refreshment which Lucy Mouse offered.

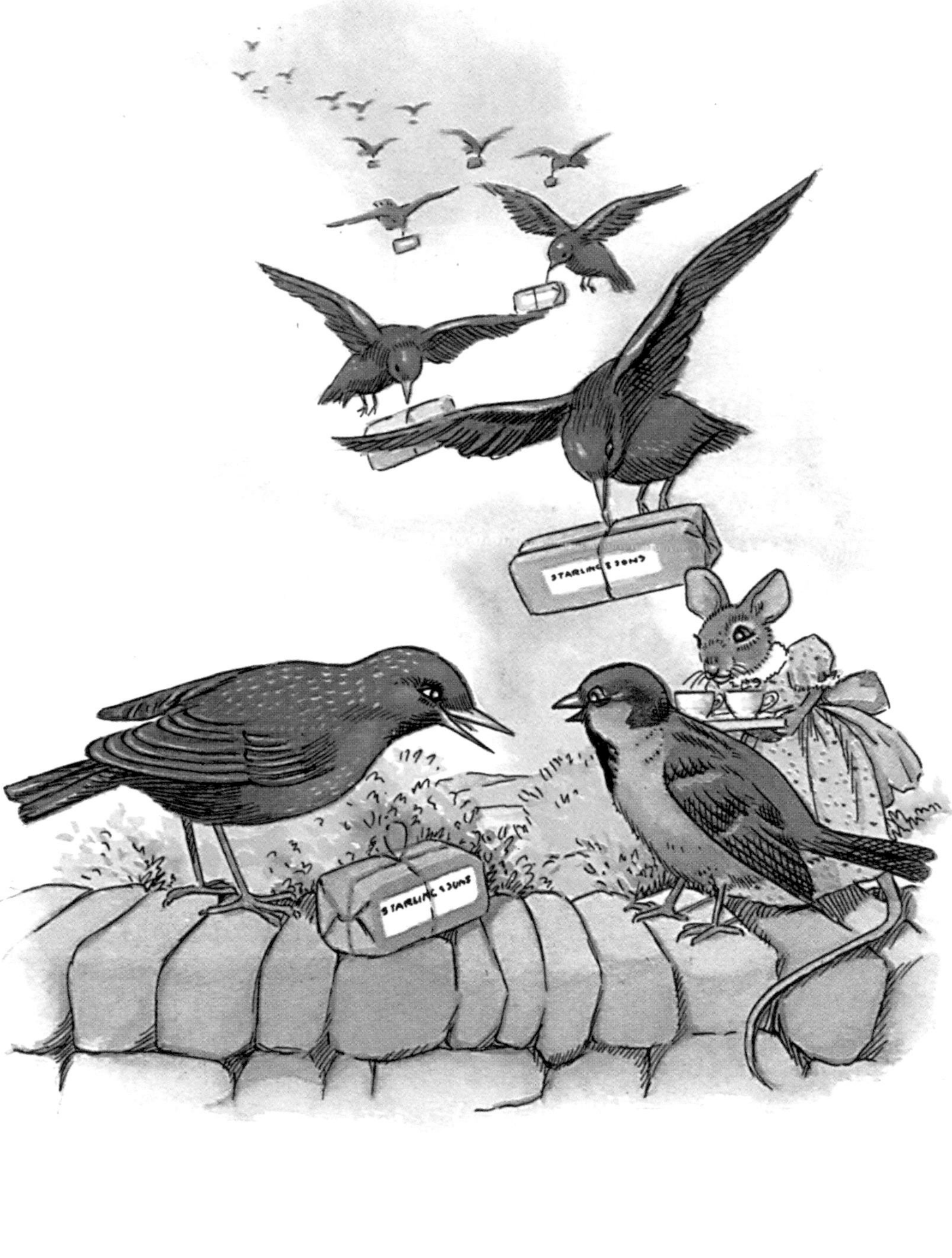
STARLING & SONS
STARLING & SONS

SAM SPARROW'S SHOP
COME IN

That evening Ernest Owl came
round to the shop with a present.
It was a notice he had made to go
over the shop. Sam was very
proud, and thanked Ernest Owl
very much. Between them they put
it up.

The next day Sam opened his shop
and looked proudly at the shelves
full of all the things he thought
Blackberry Farm would want.

SWEETS

CHEESE

BISCUITS

CARROTS

SOAP

PENCILS

BAKED BEANS

and many other useful things
as well.

All the Blackberry Farm animals
came to buy. They brought their
shopping bags and their baskets
and their purses. And they bought
so much that in the evening Sam
Sparrow had to send another
letter to Mr Starling, asking him
to come again as soon as possible.

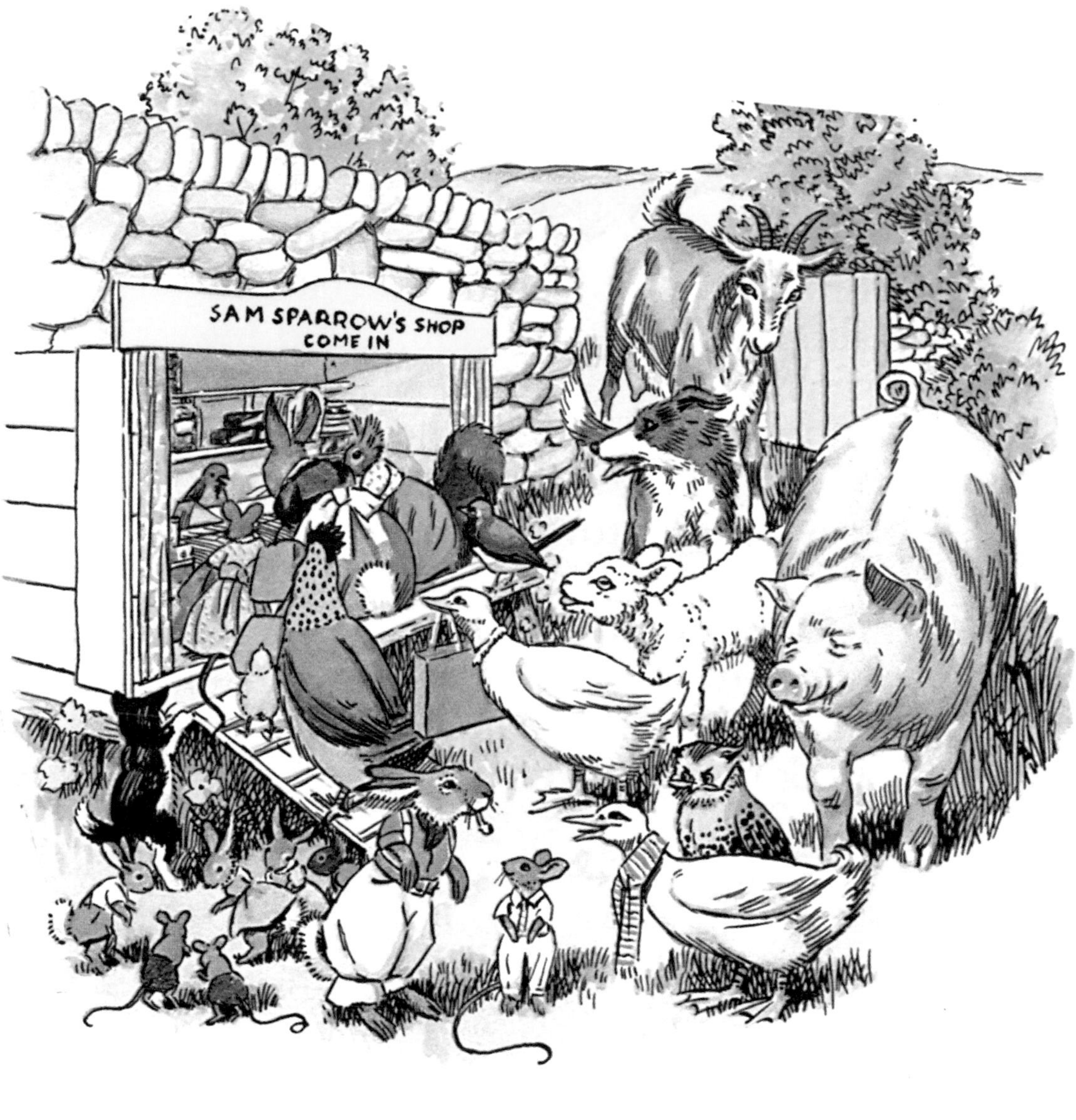
SAM SPARROW'S SHOP
COME IN

That night Sam and Joe and Ernest Owl talked about the new shop. "You MUST stay," said Joe and Ernest. "We need a shop at Blackberry Farm." And Sam said, "I would like to stay with you. I am really a town sparrow, but I was tired of the noise and all the new building and just had to get away from it all." So Sam stayed, and his shop became a very important part of life at Blackberry Farm.

SAM SPARROW